Sinead
the Dancer

Anna Donovan

• Pictures by Susan Cooper •

THE O'BRIEN PRESS
DUBLIN

First published 1998 by The O'Brien Press Ltd,
12 Terenure Road East, Rathgar, Dublin 6, Ireland.
Tel: +353 1 4923333; Fax: +353 1 4922777
E-mail: books@obrien.ie
Website: www.obrien.ie
Reprinted 1999, 2000, 2004, 2006, 2012, 2015.

ISBN: 978-0-86278-571-0

7 9 10 8

15 17 18 16

Typesetting, design, layout and editing: The O'Brien Press Ltd
Printed and bound in Ireland by Clondalkin Digital Print.
The paper used in this book is produced using pulp from managed forests

The O'Brien Press receives assistance from

Can YOU spot the panda
hidden in the story?

'I want to learn dancing,'
said Sinead.
She hopped and jumped,
and waved her arms.

'Well,' said Mum,
'that's a good start.'

'I'm going to learn dancing,'
Sinead told Dad.
'Oh!' he said. 'So you're
going to be a dancer now,
are you?'

'No!' said Sinead.

'I'm going to be a firefighter,
I **told** you that. I just want
to **learn** dancing.'

'Oh!' said Dad.

Sinead **twirled** and **twisted**, and she **tapped** her **toes**.
She **clapped** her **hands**.
She **clicked** her **fingers**.
Then she stopped.

'Music!' she said. 'I need music.'
She looked through
Mum's discs.
There was Spanish music.
There was Russian music.
There was Irish music.

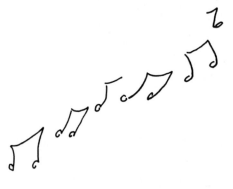

'Ah!' she said. '**Riverdance!**'
'That's it!' she said.
'I'll learn Irish dancing.'

She put on her music and
danced like Riverdance.

'**I just love dancing**,'

said Sinead.

She **swept** across the floor.

She **twirled** and **twisted**.

She **leapt** in the **air**.

She told her best friend Tom.
'I'm going to
Irish dancing class,' she said.
'Will you come too?'
'No way!' he said. 'I'd have
to wear a **skirt**!'

Mum took Sinead
to the Irish dancing class.
She asked Tom to come too
but he said no.

'You can wear your own
clothes,' Mum told him. 'You
don't have to wear a skirt –
anyway, it's a kilt.'
But he didn't believe her.

There were lots of children
at the dancing class.

There were boys and girls –
and the boys did not
wear skirts!

The children all stood in a long
line and danced together.
They made a big, loud clatter.

The new children watched.
'You will soon be able to do
that,' the teacher told them.
'Now, here we go!
Stand straight.
Hands down. **Toes out**.'

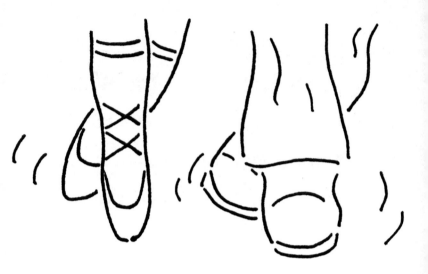

The children stood in a row
and put out their toes.
'Hop one, two, three!'
called the teacher.
They all hopped,
then stepped one, two, three
along the floor together.

All except Sinead.
Sinead **twirled** and **twisted**,
and she **tapped** her **toes**.
She **clapped** her **hands**.
She **clicked** her **fingers**.

'**Stop**!' shouted the teacher.

'That's not Irish dancing.
You must hold your arms
down like this,
you must point your toe,
you must count one, two, three.'
'Okay,' said Sinead.

Next week Tom came
to the dancing class.
He put out his toe.
He hopped.
He counted one, two, three.

But –
Sinead **twirled** and **twisted**,
and she **tapped** her **toes**.
She **clapped** her **hands**.
She **clicked** her **fingers**.
She swept across the floor.

'**Stop**!' shouted the teacher.
'Sinead! That's not Irish
dancing. I think you should
learn ballet.'

'Can I twirl and twist in ballet?'
said Sinead.

'Oh yes,' said the teacher.

'I'm sure you can.'

'I'm going to learn ballet,'
Sinead told Tom.
'Will you come too?'

'No way!' Tom said.
'I'd have to wear **tights**!
I'm staying in Irish dancing.'
And off he went,
hop one, two, three!

Next week Mum took Sinead
to ballet class.

It was full of little girls.
Some of them had frilly dresses
and they all wore white tights.
There were no boys.

The girls stood on tippy-toes
holding on to a bar.
'Hey!' said Sinead. 'That's great.
I want to do that!'

She raced over to the bar.

'Sinead!' called the teacher.
'You don't start there.
Come over here and
I'll teach you what to do.
Now, stand straight and
reach up to the sky.'

All the new girls stood and
reached up to the sky.
Sinead stood and
reached up to the sky too.

Then they bent over and
reached down to the ground.

But Sinead did not bend over.

She **twirled** and **twisted**,
and she **tapped** her **toes**.
She **clapped** her **hands**.
She **clicked** her **fingers**.
*She **swept** across the floor.*

'Yippeee!' she yelled.
'I just love dancing.'

All the girls stared.

The teacher stopped.

'Sinead!' said the teacher.
'That's not ballet.
You'll never be a ballet dancer
if you do that.'
'But I don't **want** to be
a ballet dancer,' said Sinead.
'I want to be a firefighter.'

'Oh!' said the teacher.
'Maybe you should
go to gym classes instead.'

'Hey!' said Sinead,
'that's a great idea.
Mum, can I learn gym?'

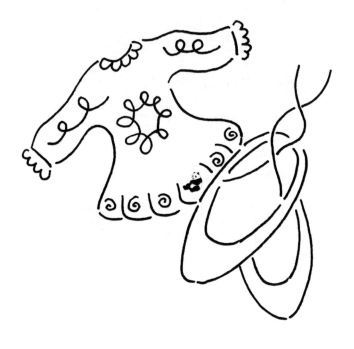

'Well,' said Mum,
'we've tried **Irish dancing**.
We've tried **ballet**.
Gym is the **very last thing**
we'll try.'

'Tom,' said Sinead,
'I'm going to learn gym.
Will you come too?'
'Would I have to wear tights?'
asked Tom.
'No way!' said Sinead. 'I think
you can wear a track suit.'

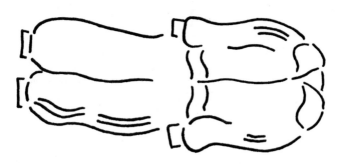

'Okay so,' said Tom. 'I'll do
gym as well as Irish dancing.'

Mum took Sinead and Tom
to the gym class.
It was full of boys and girls.

They jumped on to
a big wooden bench.
They stood on their hands.
They tumbled and rolled over.
They did cartwheels.
'Wow!' said Sinead.

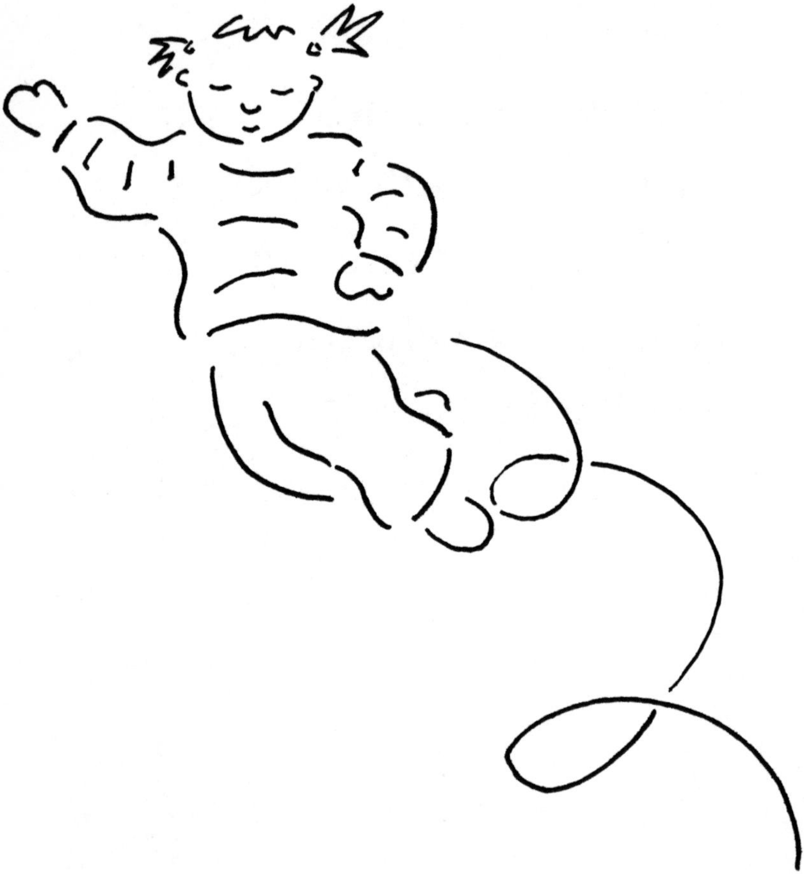

Sinead **twirled** and **twisted**, and she **tapped** her **toes**. She **clapped** her **hands**. She **clicked** her **fingers**. She ***swept*** across the floor.

'**Sinead**!' said the teacher.
'Well done! That's very good.
But I can teach you
how to do it better.'

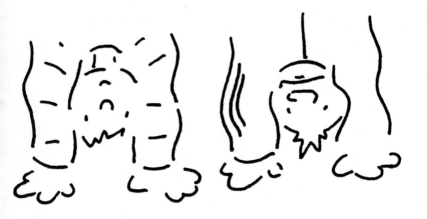

She showed the new children
how to stand on their hands.
She showed them
how to do cartwheels.

Sinead tried to do cartwheels
across the floor
but she could only do
one wobbly one at a time.
Tom kept falling over
in a heap.

'Don't worry,' said the teacher.
'You'll soon learn it.'

Sinead and Tom
practised and practised.
Soon, Sinead could do
three cartwheels in a row
and Tom could do
one wobbly one.

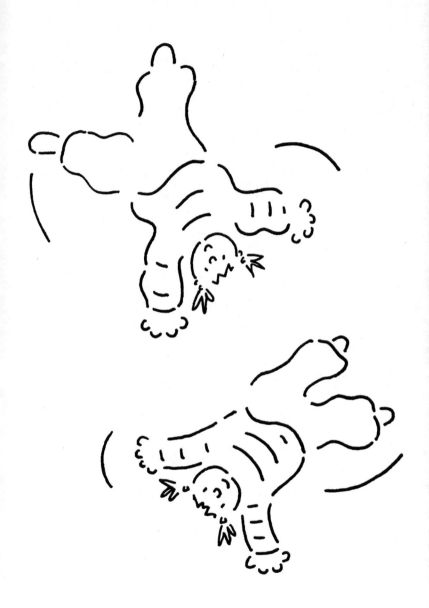

'Dad!' called Sinead. 'Watch!'
Sinead turned on the music.

She **twirled** and **twisted**,
and she **tapped** her **toes**.
She **clapped** her **hands**.
She **clicked** her **fingers**.
*She **swept** across the floor.*
She did three good cartwheels.

Tom did some Irish dancing
and a wobbly cartwheel.

'Well done,' said Dad,
and he clapped and cheered.
'Can I join in?'

'**You**?' said Sinead.
'Can you dance?
Can you do a cartwheel?'
'I can try,' said Dad,
and he smiled.

Sinead put on the music.
She **twirled** and **twisted**,
and she **tapped** her **toes**.
She **clapped** her **hands**.
She **clicked** her **fingers**.
She swept across the floor.
She did three good cartwheels.
Tom did some Irish dancing
and a wobbly cartwheel.

Then **Dad** *swept across
the floor*, tapping his toes like
hailstones falling on the roof.
He **twirled** and **twisted**.
He **hopped** and **jumped**.

He **clicked** his **fingers**
and **clattered** his **heels**
like a Spanish dancer.
He did cartwheels
right around the room.

He was

magnificent.

'Wow!' said Sinead.

'Hey!' said Tom.

'Mum!' called Sinead.

'Mum, watch this!'

Sinead put on the music

and Tom and Dad and Sinead

did it all over again.

Mum clapped and clapped.
'That was great!'
she said, smiling.

'No, it wasn't,' said Sinead.
'It was **magnificent.**
You were like a champion,
Dad.'

'Well, he was a champion,'
said Mum. 'Come on,
I'll show you his medals.'

She took a box out of a
cupboard and took off the lid.
Inside were lots of
gold and silver medals.

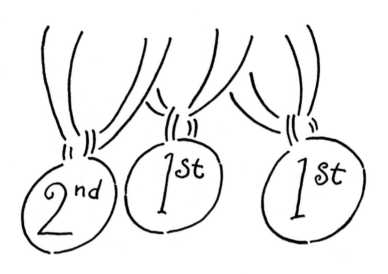

'Oh Dad!' said Sinead.
'Brilliant!' said Tom.

'I will give you
one medal each to keep,'
said Dad. 'And maybe you'll
win your own medals
some day.'

'**Yes**!' said Sinead and Tom,
and they went off to practise.

Well, did you find him?